YANKEE GO HOME

BY DEB LANDRY

ILLUSTRATED BY CHRISTINA ST.CYR

ISBN 0-9773738-0-0

Library of Congress Control Number: 2008924070

Copyright by Deb Landry, Bryson Taylor Publishing

First printed, April 2008
Edited by: Susan Gold, Custom Communications, Inc.

BTP

Bryson Taylor Publishing
Bryson Taylor Inc.
199 New County Road   Saco Maine 04072
www.brysontaylorpublishing.com

DEDICATION

To our children Cain, Drew, Cheryl, Camille, Brianna and Aleigha. Thank you for inspiring us to be the best we can be.

ACKNOWLEDGMENT

Aloha to Keonepoko Elementary School in Pahoa Hawaii and a special Mahalo to the students in Miss Lim's kindergarten class for contributing Akela's name.

FOREWORD

Yankee is a delightful poodle who is inquisitive and rambunctious like so many latch key children. Children need to be safe on so many different levels. This story is a lesson for both parents and children. Afterschool care can provide a safe environment to allow "puppies" to play and make friends under the watchful eye of adults. It allows parents to be confident that not only are their children safe, but they are also protected from loneliness and isolation.

Bullying is now recognized as a serious problem impacting children everywhere. Both support from a bystander and adult intervention are the best ways to deal with these situations. Demonstrating how this can be done appropriately in this charming story sends a clear and powerful message to a child. Deb Landry has done a masterful job blending both these themes in Yankee Go Home.

Robin D'Antona, Ed.D. Author of "101 Facts about Bullying: What Everyone Should Know"

Yankee played in the yard every day. He sniffed the flowers, rolled in the grass, and chewed on his bones. He was a happy pup, who loved to play with his toys.

But doing the same thing day after day was boring. Yankee soon grew tired of his toys. He was lonely, and he wanted to do something new.

Yankee decided to bury his bone.
He dug
            and he dug
                        and he dug.

he hole grew bigger and bigger. When he finally stopped digging,

ankee discovered he was standing outside the fence looking in!

ankee thought it would be fun to wander around and explore this

ew territory beyond his backyard.

Yankee climbed to the top of the hill and looked down into the neighborhood below. Children were playing, dogs were barking, and people were working in their yards.

Ms. Lark and Mr. Rodriguez were mowing their lawns. Yankee stoppe to watch, but Mr. Rodriguez shouted at him. "Yankee, GO HOME!" But Yankee didn't listen. He was having too much fun.

Yankee trotted down the hill and stopped in front of a big white house. A friendly mixed breed dog, named Akela was sunning herself on the front porch. Yankee barked hello, introduced himself, and wagged his tail. "Won't you come and play with me?" he asked. Akela, looked up from her nap. "Yankee," she said, "you should go home." But Yankee didn't listen. He wanted to continue his adventure.

Yankee sniffed all the mouth-watering new smells. He explored all the interesting new spots where he could play. How wonderful, he thought, to be able to go wherever I want.

Children played in a driveway nearby. When Yankee ran over, a boy tossed him a ball, and he fetched it.

Ms. Lark gave Yankee a biscuit when he passed through her backyard. "Here you go," she said. "Now, Yankee, go home." But Yankee didn't listen. He went to look for other friends. As he wandered through the neighborhood, Yankee thought of how much fun he was having. If only he could crawl under the fence every day to play with his new friends.

Down the street Yankee saw a pack of dogs huddled around a big trash can. He trotted up to the pack and barked to get their attention.

Kit, the leader, and Caboodle, his sidekick, growled at Yankee, while the other dogs circled around him. "Who said you could join in? Get lost, squirt. We don't want the likes of you hanging out with us," they said. "Go home, twerp." But Yankee didn't listen.

"Why can't I play with you?" Yankee asked, puzzled and hurt at being excluded.

"You're just a poodle," said Kit with a mean laugh. "That's a mangy breed. We only hang out with REAL dogs."

Discouraged, Yankee wandered off and soon came to Ms. Lark's yard. There he discovered another trash can just like the one Kit and Caboodle had been pawing through.

Curious, Yankee jumped up and knocked the trash can over. The can's contents spilled onto the driveway. Yankee found all kinds of treasures: bones, cookies, and many other tasty treats. Before he could eat the goodies, though, Ms. Lark shooed him away. "Go home, Yankee, before you get into more trouble than you can handle." But Yankee didn't listen.

He headed back up the street.

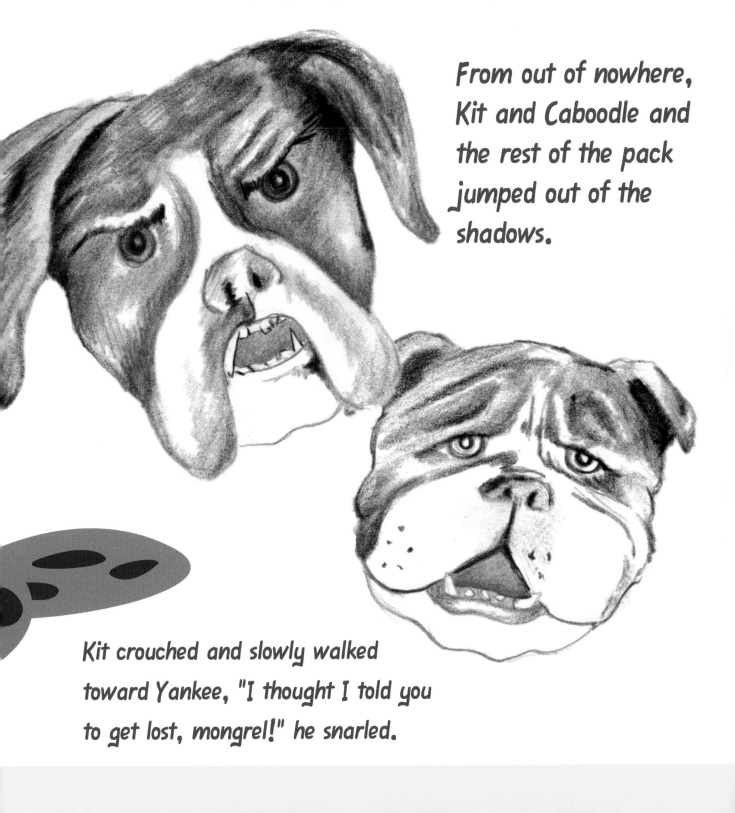

From out of nowhere, Kit and Caboodle and the rest of the pack jumped out of the shadows.

Kit crouched and slowly walked toward Yankee, "I thought I told you to get lost, mongrel!" he snarled.

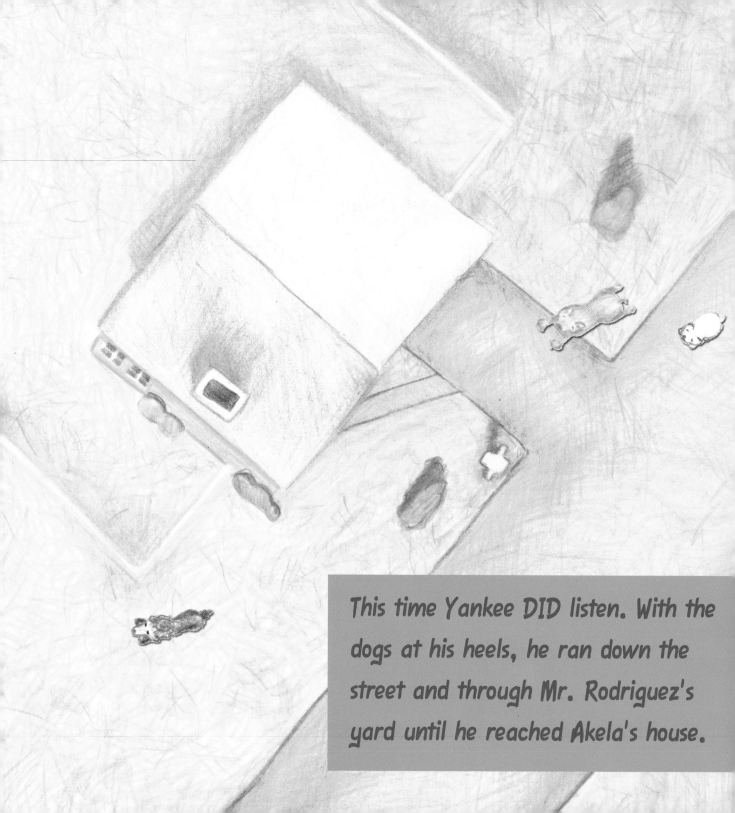

This time Yankee DID listen. With the dogs at his heels, he ran down the street and through Mr. Rodriguez's yard until he reached Akela's house.

It's not safe to wander around without your parents Yankee, you need to go home now," she said gently.

When the coast was clear, Yankee finally headed for home. He was relieved when he spotted his white picket fence. But that didn't last long!

Yankee headed for the hole under the fence, but then he froze with fear.

Kit and Caboodle were standing there waiting for him. Suddenly, Yankee wished he had never left his own backyard and never met Kit and Caboodle. "We told you to go home, Yankee," Kit taunted.

"But . . . but I am home," Yankee sputtered. He looked longingly at his toys and his dog house beyond the fence. "Well, I'm almost home," he said sadly.

Yankee cowered as the growling canines surrounded him.

e darted to the hole and tried

squeeze back under the fence.

ut Kit blocked his way. Caboodle bit at Yankee's heels and

napped at him. "You didn't move fast enough for us, mutt,"

it growled. "Now you're going to pay for snooping in MY

eighborhood!"

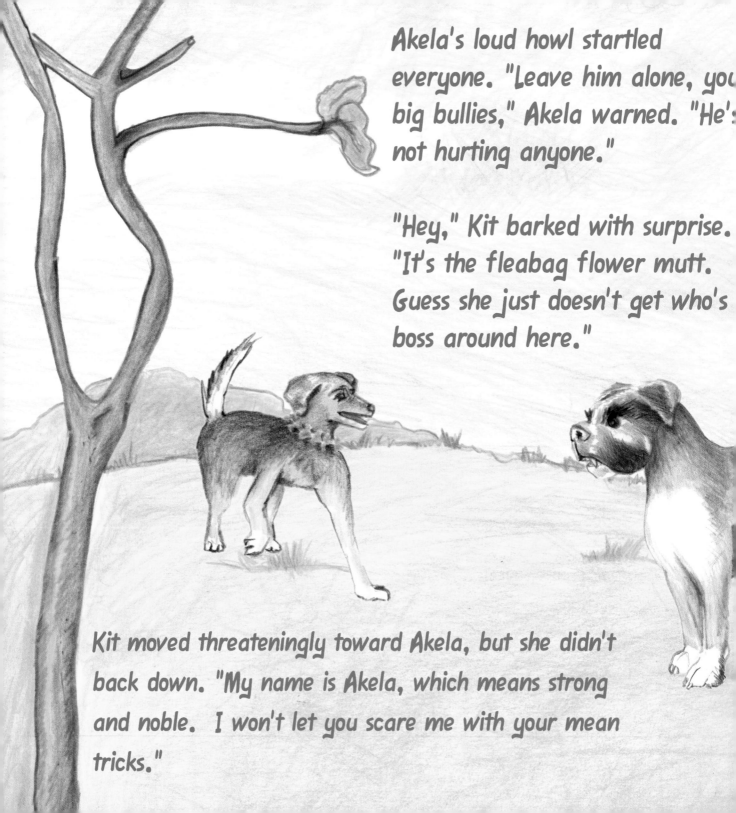

Akela's loud howl startled everyone. "Leave him alone, you big bullies," Akela warned. "He's not hurting anyone."

"Hey," Kit barked with surprise. "It's the fleabag flower mutt. Guess she just doesn't get who's boss around here."

Kit moved threateningly toward Akela, but she didn't back down. "My name is Akela, which means strong and noble. I won't let you scare me with your mean tricks."

As Kit and Caboodle began circling Akela, Mr. Rodriguez appeared. "Get out of here, you dogs," he shouted at Kit and his buddies.

The pack quickly ran down the street and out of sight. Mr. Rodriguez opened the gate and let Yankee into the backyard. Oh, it was good to be home!

When Mom and Dad returned, Yankee, Akela, and Mr. Rodriguez were waiting for them. They were concerned when Mr. Rodriguez told them about Yankee's day.

Dad filled in the hole so Yankee couldn't escape again.

The next morning when Mom and Dad left for work, they had a surprise for Yankee. He was going to doggie daycare with his new friend, Akela. After his escape, they realized Yankee shouldn't be left alone all the time.

Pawz-n-Around
Abbey
Yankee
Akela
Drew
Cain9
Gabriel
Samantha
Brianna
Aleigha
Ruby

Now Yankee and Akela play with their new friends at doggie daycare, walk safely through the park with watchful adults, and stretch out for long afternoon naps in the sun.

Yankee is no longer lonely, and he never gets bored these days. There's just too much to do!

At the end of the day, though,
he's always happy to go home.